Arlen
The Anxious
Alpaca

Hello
friends!

My name is Arlen,

I love to dance and play,

I live on a fantastic farm,

And eat mostly grass and hay.

Every sunny afternoon,

Some nice humans come by,

With lots of yummy, tasty treats,

For all of us to try.

Yet when the humans come with treats,

I don't feel happy or excited,

Instead I start to shiver and shake,

And feel so very frightened.

Then my heart, it starts to race,

I get ever so sweaty and hot.

I really don't feel like eating much,

I just freeze there on the spot!

My good friends Anna and Ava,

Say "it's the best time of the day!"

Now I'm really upset and so confused,

Why don't I feel the same way?

My friends all love the humans,

They tell me everything is ok,

But still each time I see them there,

I just want to run away!

Arlen spent a very long time,

Alone and hiding away,

He became so very lonely,

And bored of eating just hay!

Arlen felt so scared and worried,

Sometimes he sat and cried,

Until one day he decided,

He would run away and hide!

The wise and old Alpaca,

Adam was his name,

Noticed that young Arlen,

Just didn't seem the same.

Adam slowly approached young Arlen,

Who he spotted hiding behind a tree,

He asked Arlen, with a friendly smile,

"Would you like to come and sit with me?"

Adam told a wide-eyed Arlen,

That he too had felt this way,

And that going along with a friend,

Can help to take some fear away.

"The more you go and face the worries,

The easier it will get.

One day the worries you feel right now,

You will soon forget!"

Over the next few days at the farm,

Adam stayed close by Arlen's side,

It felt less scary to see the humans,

Each time Arlen tried.

Adam said "It really helps,

To focus on just one thing,

So try thinking about and focusing on,

The tasty treats the humans bring."

Adam showed Arlen tips,

To help him stay in control,

Like taking deep breaths, in and out,

Or to go for a nice long stroll.

Trying to focus on the things he can hear,

Or the things he can smell, taste, or see,

Are some of the ways Arlen has learned,

To manage his anxiety.

Using his helpful new tips and tricks,

Arlen began to smile and have fun,

So when the humans next arrived,

He no longer wanted to run.

His feelings of worry, fear, and panic,

Slowly started to come to an end,

In wise old Adam who taught him so much,

Arlen made a great new friend.

Arlen and Adam want you to know,

That these feelings aren't weird or strange,

Anxiety is very common,

Especially in times of big change.

Learning tips like Arlen has,

Can be helpful and easy to do,

So let's take a deep breath, in and out,

Now you can do it too!

It is important to remember,

That you are not alone,

You too can overcome your worries,

Just look at how much I've grown!

Tips and Tricks!

1. Breathe in for 3 counts through your nose, out for 3 through your mouth

2. Draw an imaginary square with your finger. Breathe in whilst drawing up, out when drawing across, in when drawing down, and out again when joining it up!

3. Name 5 things around you that you can see, 5 things you can hear, and 5 things you can smell

4. Think of and list 10 animals, places, fruits, or toys

5. Draw a picture or do some colouring in

6. Listen to your favourite music

7. Go out for a walk

8. Play a game

Adam

Tips for grown-ups:

If you notice your child appears anxious, here are some ways you can help:

1. Acknowledge your child's worries, reassure that it is normal to have these sometimes and that it will pass

2. Try to maintain a daily routine as this can make children feel more in control. Ensuring their daily routine includes a healthy active lifestyle and balanced diet can reduce anxiety

3. Inform your child about the symptoms of anxiety (such as feeling sick, racing heart, sweating). This can help them to identify and acknowledge their own feelings and when to ask for help

4. Leave early for events your child may be anxious for, allowing time for reassurance and distraction on the way

5. Praise steps taken to overcome worries and work together to find which tips are useful for them

If you feel that anxiety is impacting your child's functioning (for example missing school and/or events), you may wish to seek help from a professional such as their GP.

'Anxiety in Children'

NHS, (2019) -

www.nhs.uk

'Helping Your Child With Anxiety'

Young Minds, (2020) -

www.youngminds.org.uk

Printed in Great Britain
by Amazon

73019393R00020